H. Morden Bennett

Short daily meditations for Advent and Christmas

H. Morden Bennett

Short daily meditations for Advent and Christmas

ISBN/EAN: 9783741192197

Manufactured in Europe, USA, Canada, Australia, Japa

Cover: Foto ©Andreas Hilbeck / pixelio.de

Manufactured and distributed by brebook publishing software
(www.brebook.com)

H. Morden Bennett

Short daily meditations for Advent and Christmas

SHORT DAILY

MEDITATIONS

FOR

𝔄𝔡𝔳𝔢𝔫𝔱 𝔞𝔫𝔡 ℭ𝔥𝔯𝔦𝔰𝔱𝔪𝔞𝔰

BY THE

REV. H. MORDEN BENNETT, M.A.

LONDON
J. T. HAYES, 17 HENRIETTA STREET, COVENT GARDEN

1881

LONDON : PRINTED BY
SPOTTISWOODE AND CO., NEW-STREET SQUARE
AND PARLIAMENT STREET

PREFACE.

THIS little book is intended to be a help to those who wish to make a profitable use of the Seasons of Advent and Christmas, and who prefer to have thoughts suggested to them for meditation rather than formal meditations worked out for them in full.

The Advent Season is one that has a double line of teaching, as it were, prospective and retrospective,

The Church, in her Collects, Epistles, and Gospels, seems to keep both in view.

In the following helps to meditation I have endeavoured to bring both of them under consideration by making the first twenty-two meditations to have special allusion to the Second Coming of our LORD, while the remainder, including those for Christmas, bear reference to His First Coming.

The first twenty-two meditations are founded on verses in each of the twenty-two Chapters of the Revelation of S. John; those immediately preceding Christmas on the Beatitudes ; while the rest have reference to persons, places, and facts connected with the Divine Infancy.

Advent.

I. *Rev.* i. 17.   " Fear not; I am the First and the Last."

1. He who speaks is GOD.

He is also Man.

He is the first begotten Son of the Father.

But He has taken also the nature of those who were the last to be created.

2. He is the Beginning and the End of our faith :

The Beginning, from childhood up ;

The End, for He is our only future hope.

He is the Beginning and the End of our spiritual life :

The Beginning, in Baptism, when He took us in the arms of His mercy,

The End, in the Judgment, when He will be our Merciful Judge.

3. " Fear not," for

He is our Saviour as well as our Judge.

We are one with Him in our first Communion, which is our sweetest recollection ;

Our last Communion, which is our best hope.

Resolutions.—I will try to put greater confidence in JESUS.

I will try to be more submissive to His holy will.

Text (to carry away).—" It is I, be not afraid."

II. *Rev.* ii. 2. "I know thy works."

1. Our future Judge knows all our works :

Good works, under the guidance of His Holy Spirit;

Evil works under the guidance of
　　The Evil One;
　　Our own lusts and passions;
　　This wicked world.

2. We have a work to do
　　For ourselves : to work out our own salvation with fear and trembling.
　　For others : to lead them into the way of righteousness.

3. Our daily work in the world is a work for God.

No pretended spiritual work must be allowed to interfere with it.

4. All things are naked and open in GOD's eyes. He knows them.

Darkness cannot hide us.

Distance cannot remove us.

Multitude cannot distract His attention from us.

5. It is of the greatest importance what He knows about us.

On it depends our eternity.

Resolutions.—To offer every work to GOD before undertaking it.

To perform every work as unto Him.

Text.—"Commit thy works unto the LORD."

III. *Rev.* iii. 20. " Behold, I stand at the door, and
knock."

1. GOD cannot enter our hearts unless we open
to receive Him.

Sin has closed our hearts.

Repentance alone can open them.

2. JESUS stands knocking.

He stands to show His power to help, as He
stood at GOD's right hand to help S. Stephen.

But we must unbar the door ourselves before
He will help us.

And yet even repentance itself is GOD's gift,
and we must ask Him for it.

3. JESUS knocks
> By His holy Word;
> By His ministers ;
> By various events in our lives, such as sick-
> ness, death of friends, special mercies, &c.

4. If He were to enter He would bring our
souls health, strength, happiness, and at last, to
soul and body too, eternal life. .

Surely it is worth while to take some trouble
to let Him in.

Resolutions.—I will make more real efforts
after a true repentance.

I will be more careful about daily self-exami-
nation.

Text.—" LORD, I am not worthy that Thou
shouldest come under my roof."

IV. *Rev.* iv. 1.   "Behold, a door was opened in
heaven."

1. JESUS is Himself the Door.

He is the only Way, and through Him alone
we have access to the Father.

2. The atonement which He wrought has
opened this door.

He has entrusted His ambassadors with the
keys.

3. If we wish to enter by this door we must
"knock, and it shall be opened."

We must knock

> By prayer, faithful and constant;
> By communions, frequent and fervent;
> By meditations and aspirations.

4. We can see glimpses of future glory through
this door.

Let us not have at the last to cry in vain:
" LORD, LORD, open to us."

If we watch, with loins girded and lamps
burning, we may enter in by it into the city.

Resolutions.—I will try by every means to
knock more earnestly.

I will watch and be ready always.

Text.—" To him that knocketh it shall be
opened."

V. *Rev.* v. 12. " Worthy is the Lamb That was slain."

1. Worthy of what ?   Of all power, and honour, and glory.

And why ?   For He was slain for us.

This is why all men praise Him.

2. He is the Lamb slain from the foundation of the world.

He was fore-ordained to deliver us.

3. Sacrifice was always essential to true religion.

Christ's sacrifice was foreshadowed of old.

It is commemorated now.

Our worship is one with that of Heaven.

Therefore we pray : " Lamb of GOD, That takest away the sins of the world, have mercy upon us."

Life here is a preparation for eternal life.

Therefore worship here is a preparation for heavenly worship.

Therefore it should be made as like it as possible.

It should be bright, beautiful, and full of meaning.

Yet toned with sadness for our sins.

Resolutions.—To make public worship a greater reality to me.

To think of it as one with, and preparatory for, that of Heaven.

Text.—" Behold the Lamb of GOD."

VI. *Rev.* vi. 16. "Hide us . . . . from the wrath of the Lamb."

1. What a paradox—the wrath of the Lamb!
Yet it is He who once said : " Come unto Me, all ye that labour," Who will then say : " Depart from Me, ye cursed."

2. Perfect mercy and perfect justice meet in Him.
Perfect mercy now.
Perfect justice then ;
Yet tempered with mercy.

3. But how terrible will He be to the wicked !
They will long to hide from Him, but will be unable.
Justice must take its course.

4. If we seek Him as the Lamb of GOD now Who taketh away our sins, we shall not be afraid to stand before Him at His coming.

Resolutions.—I will seek after GOD now, while I have the time.
I will make special preparation for death and judgment at certain seasons.

Text.—" Be ye . ready : for in such an hour as ye think not the Son of Man cometh."

VII. *Rev.* vii. 17. "The Lamb Which is in the midst of the throne shall feed them, and shall lead them."

1. The Lamb of GOD will be the centre of worship to His saints to all eternity.
Upon Him they will depend for happiness.

2. They have learnt to feed on Him here in His Blessed Sacrament;
They will have full fruition there.
They have learnt to follow Him here;
They will be led by Him there, and follow Him whithersoever He goeth.

3. Here the Lamb of GOD was in the midst of the Cross.
There He is in the midst of the throne.
So have we to bear our cross here that we may sit down with Him in His throne.

4. We must learn, then, to follow Him through trouble and suffering, and to feed on Him in the Blessed Sacrament, that we may be numbered with His saints in glory everlasting.

Resolutions.—To follow JESUS through everything, in life and death.
To make my Communions more real.

Text.—"He shall feed me in a green pasture: and lead me forth beside the waters of comfort."

VIII. *Rev.* viii. 13. " Woe to the inhabiters of the earth ! "

1. At the last great day, when " the elements shall melt with fervent heat " :

Then will there be woe to the inhabiters of the earth.

Then will there be no more chance of repentance, for the day of grace will be past. ·

2. What will that woe mean ?

Separation from GOD and from Heaven.

The companionship of Satan and his angels.

Eternal misery and torment.

3. We know not whether we may not be of the number of the lost.

Therefore we must take great heed to ourselves.

We must not be of the earth, earthy.

We must have our citizenship in Heaven ; our hopes and our treasure must be there.

Then we shall not be consumed with the ungodly inhabiters of the earth.

Resolutions.—To " agonise " to enter in at the strait gate.

To avoid, as far as possible, the temptations of the world.

Text.—" Here have we no continuing city."

IX. *Rev.* ix. 4. "And it was commanded them that they should . . hurt . . . only those men which have not the seal of GOD in their foreheads."

1. The seal of GOD is His mark impressed by sacramental grace.

Those who have it and keep it cannot be hurt by the powers of evil.

But those who have it not, and those who have lost it, are under GOD'S wrath, and will be punished, either in this world or in the world to come; either with many stripes or with few stripes.

2. This mark, when almost lost even, may be renewed:

Only by repentance, consisting in
Sorrow for sin;
Confession of sin;
Amendment of life.

3. GOD will restore His mark by Absolution and Holy Communion to those who are truly penitent.

Resolutions.—To stir up the grace already given to me.

To repair what is weak or lacking by daily repentance.

Text.—"His Name shall be in their foreheads."

X. *Rev.* x. 5, 6. "The angel .... sware by Him that liveth for ever and ever .... that there should be time no longer."

1. Time and eternity are two totally distinct things.

Time, however long, is nothing at all compared with eternity.

Eternity cannot be measured even by millions of years.

2. There was once no time.

There will be hereafter no time.

GOD alone is from eternity.

But men also will be to eternity.

How they will spend it depends on how they spend time.

3. GOD dwells in eternity now.

With Him is no past or future.

All is one continuous present.

The Fall, the Atonement, the Judgment are seen by Him at one glance.

4. How short must our lives, for which many sacrifice eternity, appear to Him with whom a thousand years are but as yesterday !

Time will end on the Judgment Day, and eternity will then begin for us also.

Resolutions.—I will try to use every moment.

I will spend my time with eternity always in view,

Text.—"Behold, Thou hast made my days as it were a span long."

XI. *Rev.* xi. 15. "The kingdoms of this world are become the kingdoms of our LORD, and of His CHRIST."

1. In a sense, they are so now.

The Great Powers of the world are nominally Christian.

Heathen Rome became Christian, and then made way for other Christian Powers.

2. In another sense they have not yet become so.

Satan still reigns supreme over vast tracts of the world; and even in nominally Christian lands he has great power,

3. Well may we long for the time when all his power shall cease.

Then all the kingdoms of this world will be subject to GOD and to His anointed One.

This is what we should pray for.

We must pray continually, "Thy kingdom come," and we must try to spread that kingdom in every way that we can.

Resolutions.—I will pray more for, and will give more to, mission work.

I will offer myself continually to GOD, to use me, as He shall see fit, for the good of others' souls.

Text.—"Alleluia : for the LORD GOD Omnipotent reigneth."

XII. *Rev.* xii. 11. "They overcame him by the Blood of the Lamb, and by the word of their testimony."

1. The martyrs, who have given their lives for a testimony to the truth, will exult in the final overthrow of Satan.

2. Satan is called "the accuser of the brethren," for He first tempts men to sin, and then accuses them, and tries to make them despair.
He is already overcome.
But his final overthrow is reserved for the last day.
It is certain to come.

3. The saints of old overcame him.
We may overcome him too.
But not in any strength of our own.
But by the power of the Lamb of GOD.
By virtue of His death and precious blood shed for us on the Cross.

Resolutions.—To fight against Satan with full confidence of victory.
To take the saints and martyrs as examples.

Text.—"To him that overcometh will I grant to sit with Me in My throne."

XIII. *Rev.* xiii. 10. "Here is the patience and the faith of the saints."

1. Patience and faith are necessary qualities of saints.

Patience to endure hardships and persecutions.
Faith to look beyond the things that are seen.

2. The enemies of souls will at last be removed and punished.

The saints know this, and they can patiently wait for GOD's time.

They believe in GOD, and therefore they trust themselves, soul and body, to Him.

3. Now is the time to practise these virtues.

Hereafter there will be no occasion for either of them.

4. We have the saints for our examples.

We have a higher example in the King of Saints.

5. The Judgment Day will bring its full reward to those who have waited patiently and in faith for the kingdom.

Resolutions.—To strive after patience.
To trust in GOD through everything.

Text.—"Let us run with patience the race that is set before us, looking unto JESUS."

XIV. *Rev.* xiv. 1. "Lo, a Lamb stood on the Mount Sion."

1. He Who was raised up on Mount Calvary now stands on Mount Sion.

With Him are the hundred and forty-four thousand innocent ones.
They follow Him whithersoever He goeth.

2. Our LORD is shown as a Lamb to represent the Victim.
He is shown standing as the Priest.
He is on the holy mountain of sacrifice.

3. To us, measuring by time, His sacrifice appears past.
  But to S. John, gazing into eternity, He was the Lamb slain from the foundation of the world.
And he was also, as the Lamb, the centre of heavenly worship in what appears the far future.

Resolutions.—To think often of our LORD as the Lamb of GOD slain for me.
To offer Him to the Father.

Text.—"Christ was once offered to bear the sins of many."

XV. *Rev.* xv. 3. "Great and marvellous are Thy works, LORD GOD ALMIGHTY."

1. This is called the song of Moses and of the Lamb.

It is sung by the redeemed in heaven.

It is a song of praise to GOD—
For His works in creation.
For His works of grace.
For His holiness.
For His justice.

2. We hope to join in that song one day there.

We must therefore learn it now here.

Thankfulness is a duty.

Praise is a most important form of prayer, which we dare not neglect.

3. We, too, thank GOD for creation, preservation, and all the blessings of this life.

And, above all, we thank Him for the gifts of grace and hope of glory offered us through our LORD JESUS CHRIST.

Resolutions.—To strive after a thankful heart.

To make good use of the great Thanksgiving Service of the Church.

Text.—"Praise Him in His noble acts."

XVI. *Rev.* xvi. 7. " Lord God Almighty, true and righteous are Thy judgments."

1. " True and righteous are Thy judgments " in this world in the end, though evil may seem to prosper for a time.

True and righteous will be the Last Judgment, when every man will receive according to that he hath done.

True, for it is the Truth Who judges.

Righteous, or "just," for it is Justice Itself Who judges.

2. All judgment that we form must be more or less untrue and unrighteous.

Because we cannot know all the circumstances nor enter into the special temptations and trials of others.

Because, if we were tempted in the same way exactly, it is quite possible that we too should be found wanting.

Resolutions.—I will try to give up forming rash judgments of others.

I will try to be more patient and to "judge nothing until the Lord come."

Text.—"Just and true are Thy ways, Thou King of Saints."

XVII. *Rev.* xvii. 14. "He is LORD of lords and King of kings."

1. It is of the Lamb, the Son of GOD, that these words are spoken.

All power is in Him as GOD.

All power is given to Him as Man.

2. All power comes from Him.

Earthly rulers and all in authority are to be obeyed on this account.

But He must be obeyed on His own account:

Either willingly, now and hereafter;

Or unwillingly, now and hereafter.

None can resist His will in the end.

3. Our free will allows us to disobey Him.

But it cannot hinder His justice.

Far better is it, therefore, to offer Him a willing service which will meet with a reward than to be punished by Him for disobedience.

4. He reigned with the Father in eternity.

He reigned also "from the tree."

"He must reign till He hath put all enemies under His feet."

He will reign for ever and ever.

Resolutions.—To submit my whole self, body, soul, and spirit, to Him.

To submit myself to all in any way set over me "as unto the LORD."

Text.—"Thy kingdom come."

XVIII. *Rev.* xviii. 4. "Come out of her, My people, that ye be not partakers of her sins."

1. JESUS calls us to be not of the world, although in it.

We must not love the world nor the things of the world.

We must come out—

By flight from temptation;
By guard over the senses;
By prayer and faith.

2. The world and those who are of the world are reserved for destruction.

But, when we see the signs of the end approaching, we are to lift up our heads, for our redemption draweth near.

So the same event will bring destruction and salvation.

3. JESUS alone is the Rock of our salvation.

To Him we may flee and be safe for time and for eternity.

He is to be found in the Blessed Sacrament of His Body and Blood.

Resolutions.—To be not too much occupied with the things of this world.

Always to look to JESUS for help.

Text.—"Looking unto JESUS, the Author and Finisher of our faith."

XIX. *Rev.* xix. 7. "The marriage of the Lamb is come, and His wife hath made herself ready."

1. The Bride, so long betrothed, will at last espouse her heavenly Bridegroom.

She will then have made herself ready for Him.

The Church will then appear all glorious.

They who are waiting with loins girded and lamps burning will go in to the wedding.

2. Now the Church is—

Trampled on by the world ;

Abused by unbelievers ;

Rent and torn by heretics and schismatics.

But then she will be without spot or wrinkle or any such thing.

Neither will there be any more divisions nor differences, for all will be one in CHRIST JESUS.

Resolutions.—To do all in my power to help to restore the unity of the Church.

To pray for unity frequently.

Text.—" Blessed are they which are called unto the Marriage Supper of the Lamb."

XX. *Rev.* **xx.** "I saw the dead, small and great, stand before GOD; and the books were opened."

1. All will be there.

They who have served GOD, and they who have served Him not, small and great, rich and poor, wise and ignorant, young and old.

2. No false excuses will serve them.

The books will be opened in which all they have thought, and said, and done, is recorded.

They will be the witnesses for or against them.

3. The Son of GOD, Who is also Son of Man, will Himself be our Judge.

We have the Same now as our Saviour.

Our only hope of escaping His justice then is to flee to His mercy now.

He hath given power to His ministers to declare to His people, being penitent, the absolution of their sins.

So that we may come boldly unto the throne of grace.

Resolutions.—To think frequently of the Last Judgment.

To seek for pardon while I can.

Text.—"We must all stand before the Judgment Seat of CHRIST."

XXI. *Rev.* xxi. 1. " I saw a new heaven and a new earth : for the first heaven and the first earth were passed away."

1. When the present earth with all its surroundings shall be dissolved and melt with fervent heat, then—

Either out of it or apart from it shall be formed that new heaven and new earth wherein dwelleth righteousness.

Then will be seen the holy city, new Jerusalem, which S. John describes, adorned as a bride for her husband.

2. With all that is old will have passed away all that is evil.

The new Creation will be even fairer than the old, and there will be no fear of another Fall to mar it.

Resolutions.—I will strive to set my treasure and my affections above.

I will make it a subject of frequent rejoicing that I am an heir of that future glorious kingdom.

Text.—" Behold, I make all things new."

XXII. *Rev.* xxii. 20. "Surely, I come quickly."

1. Quickly, and yet the world has waited nearly nineteen centuries.

But to Him a thousand years are but as yesterday.

2. And now we are certainly very much nearer, and probably very near, to the time of His second coming.

Many signs foretell it :

Much running to and fro and knowledge increased.

The Gospel spreading rapidly into all nations.

The Jews meditating a return to their own land, &c. &c.

3. But still, in spite of these and other warnings—

He will come as a thief in the night.

Men will not be expecting Him, and He will take them unawares.

Resolutions.—To watch for the signs of His coming, and to be ready at all times.

To warn others to be ready.

Text.—" Even so, come, LORD JESUS."

𝔗𝔥𝔢 𝔅𝔢𝔞𝔱𝔦𝔱𝔲𝔡𝔢𝔰.

DECEMBER 16.

1. " Blessed are the poor in spirit: for theirs is
   the kingdom of heaven."

Who cometh? One Who was truly poor in
spirit; Who emptied Himself and made Himself of
no reputation; Who chose a lot of poverty and of
reproach and contempt; Who sought not Himself, but us.

To whom doth He come? To one who,
though miserably poor as regards the true riches,
yet thinks himself well provided and needing
nothing; to one who sets his heart on the perish-
ing things of this world to the neglect of heavenly
riches.

Wherefore doth He come? To teach me to
be poor in spirit, that through His poverty I may
become rich with the true riches which He has to
bestow.

To give the richest gift of all—Himself—in
the Blessed Sacrament of His love.

Resolutions.—To think less of myself, of my
abilities, and my rights.

To be ready to embrace outward poverty if
need be.

Text.—" What hast thou that thou didst not
receive? "

December 17.

2. " Blessed are they that mourn: for they shall
be comforted."

Who cometh ? A man of sorrows, and acquainted with grief ; One Who mourned over sin
and its consequences, and over men's rejection of
Him ; One Who knows how to comfort the
mourner.

To whom doth He come ? To one who often
mourns over the consequences of his sins, but
seldom over the sins themselves; to one who in
his grief often turns from the only source of con-
solation to the world which cannot truly comfort.

Wherefore doth He come ? To teach us for
what we ought to mourn, viz. for offending God.

To comfort us by His great gift of Himself,
and by promises of eternal joy and glory.

Resolutions.—I will mourn more over my sins
as having crucified my Lord.

I will look to Him alone for comfort in His
Sacraments.

Text.—" I will give you another Comforter,
even the Spirit of Truth."

DECEMBER 18.

3. "Blessed are the meek : for they shall inherit the earth."

Who cometh ? One Who was a perfect pattern of meekness.

" The man Moses was very meek," and so was a type of the Man CHRIST JESUS.

The meekness of CHRIST made Him silent when falsely accused and smitten.

He did not even, with His Apostle, exclaim : " GOD shall smite thee, thou whited wall," but was as a lamb led to the slaughter.

To whom doth He come ? To one who loves to have his own way, and can brook no contradiction ; who is often ready to return an injury, and forgetful of his duty of returning good for evil.

Wherefore doth He come? To teach me to turn the left cheek to him that smites on the right.

To set me an example of meekness, both by His life on earth and by His utter self-abasement in the Eucharist.

Resolutions.—To try to be more forbearing, and to be prepared for slights and contradictions.

To humble myself with my LORD, as a co-heir with Him, not of earth only, but also heaven.

Text.—" The meek-spirited shall possess the earth."

DECEMBER 19.

4. "Blessed are they which do hunger and thirst
    after righteousness: for they shall be
    filled."

Who cometh? One Who is ever hungering
and thirsting after my salvation and that of the
world; One Who has ever hungered and thirsted
after doing His Father's will; One Who longs for
me to hunger and thirst in the same way.

To whom doth He come? To one who has a
great desire after worldly things, but a very feeble
wish for things above; to one who has but little
responded to the ardent desires of His LORD for
his salvation.

Wherefore doth He come? To be born on
earth, to suffer, and to die for my salvation.

To bring that salvation to me in His Blessed
Sacrament.

Resolutions.—To have a greater desire for my
own salvation, and that of others.

To hunger and thirst after JESUS CHRIST in the
Blessed Sacrament, that I may be filled with
Him.

Text.—" Ho, every one that thirsteth, come ye
to the waters!"

December 20.

5. " Blessed are the merciful : for they shall obtain mercy."

Who cometh ?   The merciful One, our Saviour, our only Help in time of need ; One Who was ever going about doing good when on earth ; One Who will not break the bruised reed.

" His mercy is over all His works," and He is merciful even " to the unthankful and the evil."

To whom doth He come ?   To one who sorely needs mercy, but who feels not his need as he should ; to one who, when forgiven his great debt, is but too ready to demand the hundred pence from his fellow-servant.

Wherefore doth He come ?   To be merciful to our souls and bodies too, when He might justly destroy both.

To bestow mercy through Sacramental channels ; nay, to come Himself, "and heal us."

Resolutions.—To be ready to forgive others as I would have forgiveness at God's hands.

To seek for mercy, and still more for the Merciful One.

Text.—" Mercy rejoiceth against judgment."

DECEMBER 21.

6. "Blessed are the pure in heart: for they
   shall see GOD."

Who cometh?   One infinitely pure, Who is
" of purer eyes than to behold iniquity"; One born
on earth without spot of sin of a pure Virgin;
One in Whose sight the very stars are not pure.

To whom doth He come?   To one originally
born in sin, and now defiled by many actual sins
of his own; to one who can with difficulty keep
his body under and restrain his tongue from evil.

Wherefore doth He come?   To sanctify water
to the mystical washing away of sin, and say to
the penitent: " Thy sins be forgiven thee."

To give His own most pure Body and Blood,
that our sinful bodies may be made clean, and our
souls washed.

Resolutions.—To strive and to pray for purity
of heart, that I may see GOD.

To receive the Blessed Sacrament frequently
with this intention.

Text.—' Thine eyes shall see the King in His
beauty."

December 22.

7. " Blessed are the peace-makers : for they shall be called the children of God."

Who cometh ? The Prince of Peace ; Who loves peace and hates strife ; Who can give us such peace as the world cannot give.

To whom doth He come ? To one who has " without fightings, within fears " ; to one who, though called a child of God, has done little or nothing to deserve it by making peace.

Wherefore doth He come ? To make peace by the covenant of His own Blood between man and God.

To bestow the peace of God which passeth all understanding through our reception of that same most precious Blood.

Resolutions.—I will strive to " live peaceably with all men," and to be a peace-maker.

I will keep apart for a little, always if possible, after Communion, in order to realise the peace which Jesus brings.

Text.—" Behold, how good and joyful a thing it is, brethren, to dwell together in unity."

December 23.

8. "Blessed are they which are persecuted for righteousness' sake : for theirs is the kingdom of heaven."

Who cometh ? One Who was Himself persecuted for righteousness' sake ; One to Whom the kingdom of heaven of right belongs, and Who can give it to whomsoever He will; One Who has bidden us take up our cross and follow Him.

To whom doth He come ? To one Who has but little of the spirit of a martyr; to one who, being very far from righteousness, deserves far worse things than are ever inflicted on him.

Wherefore doth He come ? To open the kingdom of heaven to all believers.

To give strength to bear persecutions and afflictions, and grace to attain to the heavenly kingdom through His Blessed Sacrament.

Resolutions.—To look to the martyrs, and above all to the Chief of the Martyrs, for example under trial.

To seek for that Divine grace which supported them, humbly and earnestly.

Text.—"They persecute me falsely; oh, be Thou my Help!"

DECEMBER 24.—VIGIL OF THE NATIVITY.

9. "Blessed are ye, when men shall revile you, and persecute you, and shall say all manner of evil against you falsely, for My sake . , . great is your reward in heaven."

Who cometh ? The High and Holy One Who inhabiteth eternity. The King of Israel in the Name of the LORD. The Man of sorrows and acquainted with grief.

And these three are One.

To whom doth He come ? To one who professes the Name of CHRIST, but often does things unworthy of that Name ; to one who cannot bear to be evil spoken of, yet is too ready to accuse others.

Wherefore doth He come ? To set us an example, that we should follow His steps.

To give us His Divine Presence to be with us, that under the shadow of His wings may be our refuge until this tyranny be overpast.

Resolutions.—To have a perpetual fear and love of GOD's Holy Name, and be more trustful in Him.

To prepare for Christmas Communion with special remembrance of the Divine Presence and of our refuge with Him.

Text.—"Blessed is He that cometh in the Name of the LORD."

Christmas.

DECEMBER 25.—FEAST OF THE NATIVITY OF CHRIST.

THE INCARNATION.

I. " The Word was made Flesh."

Picture to yourself the inn, the stable, the manger and the Babe lying therein.

1. The Son of GOD came down from heaven and was made Man that we might ascend to heaven by being united to Him as GOD, and thus becoming partakers of the Divine nature.

2. He also came to offer the one all-sufficient Sacrifice for the sins of the whole world.

In the Blessed Sacrament we partake of the fruits of the Incarnation by being made one with Him and by feeding on that Holy Sacrifice.

Adore JESUS CHRIST in the manger and in the most holy Sacrament of the Altar.

Offer to the Father that same beloved Son of His as the only Offering truly worthy of Him.

He will give you in return more than either you can desire or deserve.

Resolutions.—To try to make my Christmas joy a spiritual reality, and not a mere thing of this world.

To make continual acts of the presence of GOD, especially at Celebrations of the Holy Eucharist.

Text.—" Immanuel, GOD with us."

Christmas.

DECEMBER 26.—THE BABE OF BETHLEHEM.

II. " Ye shall find the Babe wrapped in swaddling clothes, lying in a manger."

Picture.—The manger; the Infant JESUS; Angels around Him.

1. The Almighty power of GOD is humbled to the weakness of a little human Child.

And yet He becomes even more powerful to save by thus taking a weak human Body in which to suffer.

2. " He that humbleth himself shall be exalted." This is true of us too, both for time and for eternity.

Humility will lead us to the highest glory as it led Him.

Adore the Infant Saviour, with the adoring angels round His cradle. Offer Him yourself as the best birthday gift you can offer. He will give you Himself in return, the highest and most blessed Gift that He can give.

Resolutions.—To keep very near to JESUS in thought this Christmas.

To try to feel my unworthiness of that blessed Gift that He gives.

Text.—" Mine eyes have seen Thy salvation."

Christmas.

III. " Blessed art thou among women."

Picture.—The stable; the mother bending over the holy Babe.

1. The sin of the Virgin Eve, afterwards the mother of all living, is retraced by the perfect submission of the Virgin Mary, the mother of GOD.

But she has much to learn yet through suffering, for a sword shall pierce through her soul.

2. We, like her, must submit our wills to that of GOD. And we must learn obedience by the things which we suffer, after the examples of our LORD and of His mother.

Obedience will lead to a throne on high.

Adore the Infant Saviour in His blessed mother's arms.

Offer Him an entire obedience to all He bids you do.

He will, in return, make you to sit down with Him in His throne.

Resolutions.—To be always ready to follow conscience, which is the voice of GOD.

To keep, as far as possible, out of the way of temptation.

Text.—" Whence is this to me that the mother of my LORD should come to me ? "

𝕮hristmas.

DECEMBER 28.—FEAST OF THE HOLY INNOCENTS.

THE MARTYR CHILDREN.

IV. " Rachel weeping for her children."

Picture.—The scene of cruelty at Bethlehem ; Angels receiving the infant souls.

1. The Holy Innocents were Martyrs in deed, though not in will.

They had the great privilege of being the first to shed their blood for the sake of CHRIST, and also of escaping all the pollutions of this world.

And " therefore are they before the throne of GOD."

2. We pray that by the innocency of our lives, we, as they, may glorify GOD's Holy Name.

But we require something more than they did—steadfastness of faith, and that even unto death if we should have to lay down our lives for CHRIST.

Adore the Good Shepherd gathering in these little lambs, the first-fruits of His flock. Pray Him to make and keep you pure and undefiled.

Resolutions.—To become more child-like in simple trust in GOD and purity of heart.

To remember Who dwells within me, and be ready to die rather than betray Him.

Text.—" In their mouth was found no guile."

Christmas.

DECEMBER 29.—THE BLESSED FOSTER-FATHER.

V. "Joseph . . . being a just man."

Picture.—The stable; S. Joseph watching tenderly over the mother and her Divine Son.

1. S. Joseph was but a village carpenter, but he was a just and upright man, and, as such, was chosen for the highest honour that has ever been granted to a mere man, the charge of the Son of GOD and of His blessed mother.

He taught our LORD the use of the carpenter's tools, and was doubtless taught before his death by Him in return the things pertaining to the kingdom of GOD.

2. We have in him a pattern of careful attention to duties, great and small.

JESUS comes to our Altars, and dwells in our hearts.

We must guard His presence there.

Adore, with S. Joseph, the firstborn Son of Mary.

Offer Him your every-day work.

Resolutions.—To do everything as unto the LORD.

To guard, so far as I can, the Blessed Sacrament, and all things connected therewith, from irreverence, and my heart from all defilement.

Text.—"The path of the just is as the shining light, that shineth more and more unto the perfect day."

𝕮𝖍𝖗𝖎𝖘𝖙𝖒𝖆𝖘.

DECEMBER 30.—BETHLEHEM.

VI. "And thou, Bethlehem Ephratah . . . out of thee shall He come forth unto Me that is to be ruler in Israel."

Picture.—Bethlehem, a little town on the hills, but the birth-place of the great King.

1. Though LORD of heaven and earth, ruling and possessing all things, yet He stripped Himself of all and became poorest of the poor, an outcast at His birth even from the miserable shelter of a common caravanserai.

2. He became poor that we might be rich, and might be inheritors of a kingdom far more glorious than any in this world.

Adore JESUS in His poverty as much as, and even more than, on His throne of glory.

Offer Him your worldly things, as He bids you, in return for His heavenly things.

Resolutions.—I will give more in alms.

I will remember, when bowing at the name of JESUS, or at the "Incarnatus," that under no aspect is our LORD more worthy of homage than as the Babe of Bethlehem.

Text.—"Lo, we heard of the same at Ephratah."

Christmas.

December 31.—The Manger.

VII. " She brought forth her first-born Son . .
and laid Him in a manger."

Picture.—The LORD of glory lying in a manger,
with the ox and ass for His companions.

1. The incomprehensible GOD is laid in a
narrow bed in the corner of a poor stable.

Could there be greater self-abasement ?

The King of Heaven is become a subject,
the Eternal One is circumscribed by time, the
Almighty has taken the Body of a feeble Babe.

2. And this was done that we might live and
reign with Him to all eternity.

Adore the Infant JESUS as Very GOD.

Offer Him the best of your time to be spent in
His service.

He will give unto you eternal life in return
for temporal.

Resolutions.—To spend my time next year and
every year as preparing for an eternal home.

To give continual thanks to GOD the Son for
His wonderful Incarnation.

Text.—" The ox knoweth his Owner, and the
ass his Master's crib."

Christmas.

JANUARY 1.—FEAST OF THE CIRCUMCISION.

THE CIRCUMCISION OF CHRIST.

VIII. " And when eight days were accomplished
for the circumcising of the Child, His name
was called JESUS."

Picture.—The Infant Saviour brought by His
blessed Mother to be circumcised.

1. In all things our LORD fulfilled the law, and
therefore He was circumcised as a faithful Israelite.

2. But He was also circumcised to roll away
the ceremonial law by fulfilling it perfectly Himself, and therefore His name of JESUS (the LORD,
the SAVIOUR) was given then.

So that we are no longer bound by any but
the moral law.

Adore the Son of GOD become a servant for
love of us.

Ask Him to lay His easy yoke and light burden
upon you.

He will, if you bear it well, give you hereafter
a white robe and a beautiful crown.

Resolutions.—Faithfully to bear the yoke of
CHRIST, which is His Cross.

To examine myself regularly and carefully by
the Ten Commandments (which sum up the moral
law), especially before the Blessed Sacrament.

Text.—" Take My yoke upon you, and learn of
Me."

Christmas.

JANUARY 2.—THE SHEPHERDS.

IX. "There were in the same country shepherds abiding in the field."

Picture.—The hills around Bethlehem at night; the shepherds and their sheep.

1. JESUS came to the poor rather than to the rich. So His coming was announced to the poor before the rich.

These shepherds, like most of the disciples afterwards, were poor and ignorant men, but they shared the belief of their nation in a coming Messiah.

But, unlike most of their nation, they were prepared to own the Babe of Bethlehem as the Messiah.

2. We must imitate their simplicity if we would make our faith true.

Adore, with the shepherds, the Good Shepherd, who careth for His sheep.

Ask Him to seek His servant who has gone astray like a sheep that is lost.

Resolutions.—To have a low opinion of myself, and not to mind being despised if only I may find JESUS.

To love better the Good Shepherd Who giveth His life for the sheep.

Text.—"I am the Good Shepherd, and know My sheep, and am known of Mine."

Christmas.

JANUARY 3.—THE ANGELIC MESSAGE.

X. " Unto you is born this day in the city of David a Saviour, Which is CHRIST the LORD."

Picture.—The fields illuminated by celestial light; the angel communing with the shepherds.

1. This was the message that had been expected by so many generations, not of Jews only, but of Gentiles also.

2. This was the tidings of great joy that so many prophets and righteous men had desired to hear.

It caused great joy to the shepherds, and, when they had seen that great sight at Bethlehem, they returned glorifying and praising GOD.

Adore the LORD of angels and of men, Who left the ninety and nine that went not astray, and came after the one that was lost.

Ask Him for the gift of heavenly joy to cheer you.

He will give you a foretaste now, and perfect bliss hereafter.

Resolutions.—To make my religion a cheerful thing.

To be careful to make a good thanksgiving after coming to JESUS in the Blessed Sacrament.

Text.—" The LORD is my Shepherd : therefore can I lack nothing."

Christmas.

JANUARY 4.—THE ANGELIC CHORUS.

XI. " Glory to GOD in the highest, and on earth peace, good will toward men."

Picture.—The hills glowing with ineffable light; angel hosts singing praises.

1. If there is joy in the presence of the angels of GOD over one sinner that repenteth, how great must have been the joy of the angels when by the Incarnation the kingdom of heaven was opened to all believers !

2. Their joy was on account of us.

We therefore join in their song, and echo it in our Sacrifice of Praise and Thanksgiving.

Adore the Creator of all things visible and invisible, now revealed to men as the Son of Man, and worshipped by angels.

Ask Him to reveal His glory to you, as you are able to bear it, and to give you peace.

He will grant you peace on earth and glory in heaven.

Resolutions.—To praise GOD, even when He seems to have turned away His Face from me.

To remember to give special praise for special mercies.

Text.—" They made known abroad the saying which was told them concerning this Child."

Christmas.

January 5.—The Star.

XII. "We have seen His Star in the East, and are come to worship Him."

Picture.—The star in the heavens above Bethlehem; the magi travelling towards it.

1. Though CHRIST'S own people received Him not, yet Gentiles came from afar even to His cradle, led by His sign in heaven.

2. One day the sign of the Son of Man will appear in heaven, and then all the tribes of the earth will mourn on account of their sins.

Then it will be manifest who have been watching and waiting for Him and who have not.

Adore the Light to lighten the Gentiles pointed out to the magi by the light in heaven.

Ask Him to lighten your darkness, and to point out clearly the path which leads to Himself, lest you wander from the way.

He will guide you with His counsel, and after that receive you with glory.

Resolutions.—To watch for every indication of GOD's will.

To follow the light of His Word and of His Church at all times.

Text.—"Thy Word is a lantern unto my feet: and a light unto my paths."

𝔉east of the 𝔈piphany.

JANUARY 6.—THE MANIFESTATION OF CHRIST TO THE
GENTILES.

XIII. " There came wise men from the East."

Picture.—The magi travelling from afar by
difficult roads in order to worship their Incarnate
GOD.

1. The magi thought not of the length of the
journey, nor of the many difficulties they might
have to encounter.

At first probably they only knew JESUS as the
King of the Jews, yet they did not shrink from
the toil and trouble involved.

2. But we, though we know JESUS as our GOD
and our Saviour, hesitate about taking any trouble
in order to worship Him with our souls, our bodies,
or our substance.

Adore Him Who was born a King, but Whose
kingdom is not of this world.

Offer Him your gifts of love, prayer, and
contrition, and mind not the hardness of the road
that leads to Him.

Resolutions.—I will be prepared to encounter
difficulties in coming to CHRIST.

I will offer Him of my best at the Blessed Sacrament, together with my whole self.

Text.—" I found Him Whom my soul loveth."

www.ingramcontent.com/pod-product-compliance
Lightning Source LLC
Chambersburg PA
CBHW021245260626
47172CB00002B/847